AN

DISCARD

for Colin and Hilary

Copyright © 1998 by Ruth Brown
The rights of Ruth Brown to be identified as the author and illustrator of this work
have been asserted by her in accordance with the Copyright, Designs and Patents Act, 1988.
First published in Great Britain in 1998 by Andersen Press Ltd., 20 Vauxhall Bridge Road, London SW1V 2SA.
Published in Australia by Random House Australia Pty., 20 Alfred Street, Milsons Point, Sydney, NSW 2061.
All rights reserved. Colour separated in Switzerland by Photolitho AG, Zürich.
Printed and bound in Italy by Grafiche AZ, Verona.

10   9   8   7   6   5   4   3   2   1

British Library Cataloguing in Publication Data available.
ISBN 0 86264 803 3

This book has been printed on acid-free paper

Ruth Brown's
Mad Summer Night's Dream

written and illustrated by
Ruth Brown

Andersen Press • London

It was midsummer night in winter
and snow was on the ground,

When miles away, inside my head,
I heard an eerie sound.

I went down to the cellar
to look from an upstairs room,

The flowers were singing sweetly,
the birds were in full bloom.

Quite clearly in the distance,
but almost out of sight,

two fat cats were yowling,
preparing for a fight.

They were staring at each other
while sitting back to back.
One was black with brown stripes,
the brown one's stripes were black.

Three stone monkeys sprang to life,
and danced around with glee.
The blind one said, "I volunteer
to be the referee."
He said he'd watch the hissing cats
to supervise fair play —
The silent monkey by his side
said, "That will be the day!"
The other monkey next to him
said he would keep the score,
for though he couldn't hear a thing,
he'd heard it all before.

But as they started fighting
the wall came tumbling down;

The cats fell into a dried–up ditch —
I thought that they would drown.

I jumped straight in to save them,
and heard a piercing scream…

It woke me up —

— it was morning!
What a mad midsummer night's dream.